IT CAME FROM THE DARKNESS

A CHARITY ANTHOLOGY

Cover Design by Red Cape Graphic Design

www.redcapepublishing.com/red-cape-graphic-design

Cover Artwork by David Paul Harris

www.davidpaulharris.com

All proceeds from this publication go to the Max the Brave Fund

Www.maxthebravefund.org

Dedication

For Max the Brave who showed us what love is.

"It Came from the Darkness" introduction from Suzie Yardley (Max's Mum) and Lou Yardley (Max's Auntie)

Thank you for picking up a copy of "It Came from the Darkness" and supporting the Max The Brave Fund. We hope you enjoy the stories contained within these pages and we'd like you to know that your contribution is going to a very good cause.

Even though Max was only little, he did love to look at books (even if the ones his Auntie Lou writes weren't very appropriate!), so having a collection of stories to raise money for his fund seems fitting.

The Max The Brave Fund was set up in August 2019 after Max sadly passed away from a Malignant Rhabdoid Tumour (MRT, a rare childhood cancer). As Max spent most of his life in Great Ormond Street Hospital we are using this fund to help them and other organisations such as Grace Kelly Childhood Cancer Trust and Shooting Star Children's Hospices. We also help individual cases that need funds for essential treatment abroad.

You can find us online at: http://maxthebravefund.org/
http://www.twitter.com/maxthebravefund
https://www.facebook.com/maxthebravefund
https://www.instagram.com/maxthebravefund/

Thank you for your support,

Suzie Yardley and Lou Yardley

Forewords

Red Cape Publishing

We'd been working with Philip Rogers PR for a while and when he approached us with the idea for a book of drabbles and artwork, we knew it would be something special. It seemed obvious that it should be in aid of a charity, and there was no hesitation in which charity this project should support. We had been connected with horror author Lou Yardley for the past couple of years and were aware of the loss of her nephew, Max, in 2019. The family have carried out incredible work raising money for a variety of children's charities and it's a genuine pleasure to be able to help in our own way.

We decided from the outset that the project would be a secret one, enabling us to build up a degree of mystery and intrigue. It meant that we could make the anthology 'invitation-only' giving us the chance to select writers and artists we knew would be happy to be involved. Between ourselves and Phil, we contacted a huge range of authors, poets, filmmakers, actors, and scriptwriters. The response and generosity of those involved has been overwhelming and we're honoured to have some great names on the list.

We want to extend a big thanks to everyone who helped put this book together, to David Paul Harris for allowing us to use his incredible artwork on the cover, to anyone who has shared details about the book, and of course to you, the readers.

Enjoy

Peter & Leanne Blakey-Novis

Red Cape Publishing

Philip Rogers 101 PR

The original idea for this book came after reading *Armistice: 100 Days* (2018); a fantastic compilation of 100 war poems by 100 authors, all of which start and end with the same line. It was an interesting and novel concept that immediately hooked me, and I wanted to do something similar that would incorporate a cross-section of people from the horror community. So, I approached PJ Blakey-Novis of Red Cape Publishing, and after throwing around several ideas, we eventually settled on an approach to this collection. Much like *Armistice: 100 Days*, we maintained a 100-word limit, but we opened it up to a diverse range of writers and artists, inviting various contributions of stories, poems and artworks, all inspired from an opening line: It Came from the Darkness.

We gave ourselves a little over a month to get all the contributions in for the book, inviting a cross-section of talented people from across the horror community. I knew PJ–with all his experience and contacts–could bring together a brilliant group of writers. But having interviewed and worked with so many talented individuals in the horror community myself, I also hoped to bring in a selection of contributors, including not just writers and artists, but directors, horror journalists and even horror fans.

As a horror fan myself, to have the likes of Debra Lamb, Debbie Rochon, Mark Steensland and MJ Dixon all contribute is a dream come true. Each and every one of them has significantly impacted my life over the years, and it was an honour to have them involved in this book. The proceeds from the book are going to the Max the Brave charity fund, and I couldn't be happier. His story is one of tragic loss, but his smile throughout the time was an inspiration, and it is great to see his legacy live on in the charity.

Max the Brave covers so many of the fantastic children charities and causes out there, including GOSH, a trust very dear to me that has been nothing short of amazing in the care they have given my son after his diagnoses with Nephrotic Syndrome 8 years ago. This book is just my way of giving something back and saying thank you.

The road to publication has been a surprising journey, and I would personally like to thank all the people who have taken the time to contribute as well as those who buy a copy. Your efforts will help raise both money for the charity and awareness for such a great cause.

Phil

Contents

Human Nature

C.L. Raven

It came from the darkness. Eyes the colour of nightmares, and body odour that reeked of bad memories. Scuttling low on two legs, watching. Waiting. Legends of this evil haunted the forests and lakes; its presence announced by screams torn from victims' dying lips. Siren songs of suffering.

Their bodies disappeared.

Its third eye peeked through the undergrowth. Unblinking. Unfeeling. The executioner's hollow stare of death. It came from the darkness, a steel claw to drag the trophy to their lair, to be displayed in a glass box for the amusement of its own kind.

The curse of the human.

The Visitor

Ross Baxter

"It came from the darkness," she repeated, as she had to every psychiatrist who had seen her since her arrest.

The visitor looked around her tiny, windowless padded cell, taking in the soiled sheets and faeces-covered walls. His eyes finally came to rest on the thin, hollow-eyed woman propped up in the corner.

"It made me do it!" she screamed. "It penetrated me, raping my mind, taking me over, commanding that I kill, again and again. It demanded blood, it demanded souls. The…thing! It came from the darkness!"

The visitor moved closer, savouring the despair. "You're right. I did."

ARTIST

AIMEE LABAN

When the Earth Opened Up

C.M. Saunders

It came from the darkness, and I knew nothing would ever be the same. They used explosives to carve out huge fissures in the mountains near my house on their quest for minerals. Riches.

One night, I went there looking for fossils. I took my torch. Still, I didn't see the creature until it was too late. A fat, pale, eyeless worm-like thing a metre long coming out of a crack in the rock. I tried to run, but when I saw its teeth I froze.

They say money is the root of all evil.

I can vouch for that.

This Checkered Prison

Owen Townend

It came from the darkness: a tumbling counter, rattling me to the bone.

First, we collide with each other, then the inside of this wooden box, a board that folds in two. With its brown and black squares, it's a very old game.

Through the smallest crack of light, I glimpse the world outside, thick with dust. I have seen it through one eye, two eyes, sometimes as many as six.

This checkered prison has been shifted which means it will open again soon. When it does, I will finally take a chance and roll out to live or die…

Figment

Alain Elliott

"It came from the darkness." That was what Heather had said to her friend the next day.

The hospital was over one hundred years old and that night the power had gone out. She took the torch from her pocket, shining it down the long corridor.

Heather called out to the patient who was slowly walking away. There was no answer.

Walking faster, she couldn't get closer to the woman, but she knew the coded door at the end would stop her.

The patient reached the end of the corridor, walking straight through the wall and disappearing into the darkness.

And the Darkness Followed...

Roma Gray

It came from the darkness and the darkness followed.

It started with a sub exploring a sink hole off the coast of Florida, or so they say. A transmission problem, many had thought, then the blackness began to spread. First Miami, then all of Florida, and then the Gulf of Mexico.

A pilot, before the shadows swallowed him and his plane whole, reported the flapping of dragon wings. Then we heard no more.

Now there is only darkness and nothing we can do. I can hear its hungry, ragged breath outside of my house.

In this endless night, I weep.

Sleep

Bella Hamblin

It came from the darkness, a small sound, so quiet he could hardly hear it. Shrugging it off as a bad dream, he closed his eyes against the impenetrable blackness, silence returned. Movement beside him gave him comfort, his wife wrapped her arm around his chest, expecting warmth he pressed his back against her. She was cold, as if no blood ran through her, her icy fingers gripped tightly, her sharp nails drawing blood. He tried to move, but she held firm as the sound returned, louder now, angry, deep and frantic as she sunk her teeth into his neck.

Granny Goose

Bill 'Bloody Bill' Pon

It came from the darkness… of an old armoire that housed toys. I could only see her when looking through and clicking the lever on the View-Master… Her eyes were black. She wore a blue dress, white stockings and black shoes. I was scared to death and moved backwards. She said, "I gave them some broth without any bread; and whipped them all soundly and put them to bed…" I removed the viewer from my eyes and threw them across the room. Was she gone? All of a sudden something invisible grabbed me and dragged me into the old armoire.

Captivating Love

Philip Rogers

It came from the darkness
She opened her eyes
Wanting to scream
but in fear... paralysed

Her eyes scanned the room
He got one hand free
She saw me in the shadows
But *he* didn't see me

As my blade pierced through
the spine of his back
I could feel the blood drain
Bones start to crack

As he fell to the floor
Tears filled her eyes
Fear in realisation
It's better dead, than to be alive

Stop with your crying
Or you'll never be free
I won't hurt you no more
If you'll just stay with me

It Came From The Darkness

Tim Lebbon

It came from the darkness, a soft whisper that promised so much. I held my breath, wide eyes sightless. I'd never known such deep dark, yet I *did* know that voice. I'd heard it before, singing and raging, shouting with joy, crying in pain and grief. Its familiarity made it no less frightening. I waited another second, wishing I would hear it again to break the silence, but dreading it as well. And then as my scratching fingers broke through the velvet to the solid oak beneath, I realised the voice was mine, and it was saying, *Let me out.*

Dark

Peter Germany

It came from the darkness with flesh so dark you couldn't see it. You didn't know it was there until you felt its teeth.

That's what people say. It's hard to believe, but now I'm here, for a dare, I believe it. Everything is wrong in these caves. The air smells and tastes stale. Sound doesn't carry right. It echoes oddly, making pinpointing anything impossible. You could feel wet walls, hard rock under foot. But you couldn't see, and that was the hardest part.

Light brings them, so no lights.

Then it was there; warm, rancid breath in my face.

Blues for the Sinner

Mike T. Lyddon

Mrs. Smith enters the interrogation room. Her son sits handcuffed to a chair. Justin Smith looks up, tears in his eyes.

"Mama! I been so scared!"

She strokes her son's hair. "It's alright, son."

"I had to kill Papa and Sis cuz they were demons, Mama."

Mrs. Smith leans down and kisses her son on the forehead.

"Don't worry, mama's gonna talk to the detective." She leaves.

Justin smiles.

Detective Barnes waits outside. Mrs. Smith approaches him. She scowls. "He knows."

Barnes watches her disappear down the hall. He laughs, pulls out a cigarette, and lights it with a word.

Contact Tracing

John Ryan Howard

It came from the darkness. This animalistic urge to prey. Ross was working as a waiter. He thought of how easy it is to see a complete stranger in a cafe and find out their name by doing a brief search online. Now, thanks to the pandemic, it's his job to record the customer's address.

A knock on the door of his most frequent customer. "Ross? I was waiting for you." Ross steps through the doorway into the fatal bite. Through the fog of stars and warm blood he could see the yellow glowing eyes and shark-like teeth approach.

Stolen Colours

Carmilla Voiez

It came from the darkness, my jealousy, and extinguished all competing shades: laughing yellow, purple desire and vibrant red excitement, smothering them beneath its black shroud.

I was woken by relentless buzzing beside my pillow. A professionally sympathetic voice shattered my dreams and robbed me of hope. "We're sorry. We couldn't save her."

Behind the viewing window, my impotent tears desaturated the yellows, purples and reds of your battered flesh that someone had carefully arranged on a silver trolley. The knowledge that you made me do it was scant compensation as I drowned the sting of loneliness with amber liquid.

Copycat

Chisto Healy

It came from the darkness, but Seth didn't see it, as it remained behind him, mirroring his movements. He could feel someone there, but it shadowed him perfectly, moving where he moved, turning as he turned. He could never see it smiling behind him.

Sometimes it would touch ever so gently or whisper in his ear just to drive him mad. Even before the mirror, it matched his height and build, remaining hidden behind him.

Seth went wild, screaming, and it matched his dance, until he took the knife to his throat, and it finally stopped mimicking him.

ARTIST

CHISTO HEALY

Death Penalty

Theresa Jacobs

"It came from the darkness, so black it couldn't be seen.

But oh, I felt it." Mark shuddered, eyes wide.

The doctor nodded. "Uh-huh. And what was this, it?"
"Pure evil, in its truest form." He hissed, "*Essence.*"

"Well, Mr. Nolan, I find you perfectly sound. You've passed every test and I will not have you committed. You will be facing the death penalty for what you did to those people."

Laughter boiled from Mark's lips, his eyes rolled to the whites, his tongue cleaved in half and he leapt upon the doctor. "No Doc, you face the death penalty."

Legend

D.J. Doyle

It came from the darkness of the eerie thicket. Four travellers strayed from the known path and set up camp by the mountainside. Under the silvery moon, thundering footsteps approached, then a vociferous snarl. It pounced on the jittering campers and tore them limb from limb. Blood and entrails splattered across trees and rocks. The fire hissed from its rations of blood which slightly dowsed the flames. Screams evaporated into the callous air. A genus of grotesque decorated the camp as it chomped on a flayed arm.

The only evidence remaining was the enormous footprints that would arouse Cryptozoologists.

It Came From The Darkness

Laurence Saunders

It came from the darkness, *obscuring its intentions like a shroud.*

Turning the page, you smile.

I will roast you in sulphur, flay your skin piece by blackened piece and leave the sun to bleach your bones. I will wash you in gulfs of liquid fire. Heaven'll crack your shins and gnaw your marrow. Ravens'll scatter at your endless screams.

You stop reading the story. You hadn't expected this. Alone, you put down the book and listen.

I'm here. To cleanse myself in your blood, to taste your iron.

Pop! The bedside lamp goes out.

Come with me into the darkness.

Egress

Monster Smith

It came from the darkness...slithering across the earth on its underbelly, searching for fresh skins. The wreckage was significant and it peeled back its disfigured face, displaying its true nature. He paused, staring back at it through the shiny, glimmering arch.

Untold evil spilled forth, crawling out of the black, bottomless pit toward his world. Burnt, rotted flesh was discarded, revealing the hideous abomination just beneath the surface. He grabbed an axe in anticipation of chopping off its head, hoping the body would follow after. But what he saw looking back, scared him to death.

It was his own reflection.

Well of Madness

Joe Duncombe

It came from the darkness
and gently said my name.
I tried to ignore it,
even then it still came.

The wind touched my neck,
my hairs stood on end;
I took just a moment,
so my thoughts could blend.

Then I opened my eyes,
just a little to start.
Now to prepare my soul
and to still my heart.

When stood at the edge
of a pit-like well;
filled with dark, black, space
and no sound to quell.

I peered to the void
and was filled with sadness.
Now knowing my fate, and
that my future was madness.

Feast

Peter Hearn

It came from the darkness. Warm, cocoon-like, the creature lay dormant. To survive, it needed to get out - the creature had to climb.

The creature could hear deafening child-like noises growing louder, it sensed freedom. Feet scraped against the walls, trying to get a footing, pushing towards the light.

No one noticed the old man slumped alone, discarded fast food wrapping on the table, his eyes fixed.

The creature within prized open the old man's jaws; cracking, splintering them, widening the exit, finally awakening the creature's grim, gruesome appetite to a restaurant of happy looking meals.

A feast.

Worse Things Happen At Sea

Michael Holiday

It came from the darkness, the tiny glimmer of light on the dark horizon of the sea. She couldn't remember how many years she'd been looking out at this view, waiting for his small fishing boat to return.

Reaching the shoreline, the boat washed up in front of her. But it was empty. She turned away, with tears in her eyes. Suddenly, she felt a hand grab her shoulder. Shuddering as she felt the icy touch on her skin. When she turned around, someone was there. But she didn't see her husband, only the decay of what he had become.

Honeycomb Face

Eric LaRocca

It came from the darkness in the pit of my throat – a small honeybee the size of a dressmaker's thimble. As I rubbed the precious cargo I've carried in my stomach for nine months, my husband looked at me with a wordless question.

I smeared sweat as thick as honey dripping from my forehead, my fingers gently massaging the tiny pinhole that had sprouted in my cracked skin.

Stomach curling, I sensed my insides harden as if they were suddenly made of cooling wax – a droning chorus of larvae beginning to crawl through me, a hive finally about to burst.

Identity

Sam Mason Bell

It came from the darkness.

Some hear voices, some feel a presence, I wish it was that simple for me.

I grapple with the night, I fight monthly, I struggle to know me.

My voice stretches beyond piercing, a howling awakeness.

My body is a lock of deep fur, salvation pours through me.

Not everyone sees me, I scutter with the hounds. This is my true form and you can't say otherwise. You think I'm crazy, you see no transformation, But I truly see the radical monster I am.

The beast that'll break free, and feed once again, for me.

Infection

Justin Boote

It came from the darkness. White and silent, it fell from the night sky, landing softly, covering everything. And everyone.

The children loved it, standing with mouths wide open, letting the snowflakes fall into delighted mouths, throwing it at one another, soaking into their pores.

Their parents joined in.

The first signs came days later. Nausea, cramps, headaches. Then, the haemorrhages. From the nose, mouth, ears. The hospitals were overrun, everyone dying. The scientists and doctors couldn't understand it. The bacteria were of unknown origin.

Then, when the bacteria grew to grotesque parasites, they knew; the aliens were taking over.

Where's Mother?

Dale Parnell

"It came from the darkness."

That's what Father said when I asked about Mother. After that, he refused to talk about her, and the cellar door was nailed shut.

We lived in that house for twenty more years. I struggled to sleep through the sound of scratching at the cellar door, but you grow accustomed to things given enough time.

After Father died, I moved out, and burned our old house to the ground.

That night the faint sound of nails scratching down my bedroom door froze the breath in my lungs.

It had survived, and it had found me.

No Man's Land

Ian F. White

"It came from the darkness," were the Corporal's last words, which was quite remarkable in itself, considering the state he was in.

I had seen men succumb to much less; the muddy trenches and broken wasteland between were full of them; fly-infested bloated corpses, festering in the midday heat.

But this man's injuries were not caused by the actions of other men, they were the gory result of some unknown bestial assailant that had ripped him apart with hungry fangs and slashing claws.

I checked my service revolver and followed the trail of blood.

Shadows of Your Mind

Bazz Hancher

It came from the darkness,
from the shadows you believe it came,
evil is what you call it
but evil is not its name.

Beasts within the fields,
beasts that call your name,
feelings of pain and sorrow
burning in your brain.

The sounds of complete silence
are shouting in your head,
your prayers are for quietness
and you're wishing you were dead.

To you, death comes easily
compared to what you know,
don't torture yourself any longer
let this darkest secret go.

What came from the darkness,
from the shadows of your mind,
is the conscience,
you left behind.

SHADOWS OF YOUR MIND

ARTIST

BAZZ HANCHER

Sleep, It Whispered

M.J. Dixon

It came from the darkness, the noise. A scraping, a clawing at the wood of the door. For years he'd bothered me, Doodle, my dog. Every night I'd lock him in the living room, I'd watch his sad eyes disappear in the dark as I turned out the lights. "Sleep," I would whisper.

Yet without fail, every night, he would somehow get out and my sleepless night would be spent hearing him clawing at the door.

Tonight, the scratches are there again, but I lie in fear.
Doodle was put down a week ago.
Then it spoke.
"Sleep," it whispered.

ARTIST

MJ DIXON

It Came From The Darkness

Jamie Evans

It came from the darkness. Slow and slimy, working its way up from the abyss with inexorable and inevitable progress. It reached out into the light and took its first steps. Out from the darkness it moved into the light. It learned to survive, it learned to be vicious. With teeth and claws then fists and feet. It learned to create, it learned to use tools. It began to breed and spread, to ravage and consume. From one tiny creature in the shadow to a worldwide plague. We began in darkness and it is the darkness we still crave.

Tree

Bella Hamblin

It came from the darkness down a small passageway obscured by an ancient tree, bowed over in submission. She turned her head to try to identify the sound, desperate to be home, to be safe in bed. Something made her push the tree aside, its branches scratched her arm, warning her to turn back. Ignoring its plea, she continued, one step at a time, tentative but determined. This time the tree didn't provide a warning, this time it wrapped its bony branches around her ankles, forcing her to the ground. Then without further sound, it pulled her to her grave.

Leviathan

Gareth Clegg

It came from the darkness of space. A creature, ancient and immense, that had spent eons crossing the immeasurable void between worlds, now craved warmth. It passed by desolate balls of gas and rock until the third planet fell under its malevolent gaze.

This one teemed with life in great abundance and diversity, a feast beyond compare. But as it shrouded the world in a mantle of shadow, it wondered, *can this be just?*

Thousands of tiny fireflies streaked from the surface, blossoming around its body like star-blooms.

No, the creatures of this world were prey. Let the harvest commence.

Fame

Laurence Saunders

It came from the darkness. The earth cracked open. Out came slithering a small demon, moonlight dancing in its eye.

"Let me bed down here with you," it whispered, "for you shall be rewarded if you hold your peace."

I woke to see the furry creature curled up, gently purring beside my pillow. I took its photo. Uploaded to Instagram, it went viral, the world entranced. TV followed, me with my pet on breakfast shows around the globe.

I stroked its soft skin. It turned to me, flashing hideous teeth.

"I warned you," it hissed, gorging on my thick blood.

It Came From the Darkness

Janine Pipe

It came from the darkness.
Born in Hell.
Sent on a mission.
Reap havoc, spread its evil seed.
What fun, turning humans on each other in the name of
depravity.
But what was this?
From the gutters, it could see rape.
From the sewers, it witnessed mindless killing.
Earth was already tainted.
It evoked the worst of all humanity.
Torture, sadism, murder, child abuse.
For the first time ever, it was frightened.
It slunk back to Hell answering to Master.
Earth needs no help from us.
Humans have turned on each other.
They would end the world.
Hell was redundant.

It Only Takes One Something

Pat Higgins

It came from the darkness and it killed me stone dead.
I've got no idea what it was.
I was alive, then I wasn't.
You spend your life trying to stop something killing you.
You can eat more of something or less of something.
You wear a seat belt. Quit smoking.
You can block a million somethings to increase your
chances
of staying alive
but
it only takes one something to get through
and then you're dead
like I am.
So, what was it?
Cholesterol?
Car accident?
What?
Oh.
Seriously?
Bigfoot?
Well, I guess that's cooler than it could've been.

It Came From The Darkness

Gemma Paul

It came from the darkness. I begged my Papa to leave the nightlight on, but he said I was getting too old for one. The light would keep it away, but now…. I hear it before I see it. A pitter-patter of small feet coming for me. I lift my legs up, tucking them beneath me, pulling the covers high around my body, but it's no good. There's no hiding, no stopping it from climbing up the duvet as it crawls towards me, red eyes glowing.

Once the lights are out there's no hiding from the thing under the bed.

ARTIST

GEMMA PAUL

Two-Cloaked

Chris Lloyd

It came from the darkness, carrying these cloaked, taloned beings now standing over a stone slab, chanting incantations.

Thomas Livingstone lies securely restrained, blindfolded and gagged.

"It shall begin."

One shouts, "Eyes." They rush to a box. One retrieves the eye scoop. Thomas's eyes are out and eaten in seconds.

"Testicles." Another box, tool found, testicles removed.

Eaten. Appetite building quickly.

"Penis." Thomas screams, howling loudly as it is cut off. Blood spurting everywhere. They drink, get naked, lick each other, cut Thomas, eat him raw, their talons tearing him to shreds until only bones remain.

"It is done, fly."

These Four Walls

Paul Downey

It came from the darkness with the alarm clock coming into focus and that familiar ringing is working its way into my brain.

We have been housebound for what feels like six months now.

I'm terrified to go outside but I can't leave.

I haven't heard from Gareth for the past six hours, but I expect a groggy 'Good Morning' anytime soon.

I rise to my feet now and stumble slightly, forgetting how much I had to drink last night.

Walking into the living room I make out a figure on the chair and realise I've consumed the darkness.

Jane Doe

Russel Shor

It came from the darkness. Quietly, unnoticed at first and by the time we knew what it was, it was too late. You may think it slithered and sneaked its way into our lives, but it didn't. Rather it arrived with a loud splash of gore and gruesomeness…and sadness. I didn't realise just how serious the situation was as I knelt, taking the measurements of its first victim. A young girl broken from the inside out. A name. I must get her name. She was somebody. She was real. She had feelings and smiled and laughed. What was her name?

What Shadows Eat

Lou Yardley

It came from the darkness, made of shadows, doubt, and despair. I couldn't see its eyes, but I knew it was looking at me. Staring. Studying. Night after night, day after day, it came to me. It became all I thought about.

Sat in the centre of my room, the shadow made a noise. It may have been a growl or stomach rumble. The trouble is, I didn't know what shadows liked to eat.

I offered it my hand, but it didn't lick or bite a finger. Instead, it swallowed me whole. It consumed me.

Now I'm in the darkness.

The Vampire

David Owain Hughes

It came from the darkness and clacked along its tracks. Timothy Button, wide-eyed and grinning, boarded the famed rollercoaster. *What if there're real ghouls?* he thought, giggling.

"Vampire, take flight!" the operator screeched with laughter.

The ride reached its zenith, zoomed down the other side, thundering into its corkscrews and loops with menace. As the carriages rounded the final bend back to the station, Timothy saw a swarm of creatures descend upon the Vampire, blanketing it, the screams around him blood-freezing and real.

When he alighted, seeing fewer riders than boarded, he knew he'd never forget what he saw tonight…

Barry
or
How Preston's Biggest Johnny Cash Tribute Act Faced Death And Survived

Tony Sands

It came from the darkness, collided with the back wall of 84 Cronenberg Crescent and dropped with a thump into the compost bin. Barry Cash peeked out the kitchen door armed with a spatula as it raised its head. "You're not Kurt Neumann," it snarled.

"I'm Barry."

It lifted itself out of the bin, eye fixed on Barry.

"You might know me as 'Donny Cash'."

It stood silent, still.

"Preston's biggest Johnny Cash Tribute act. Ever."

"Why are you holding a spatula?" It asked.

"Flies," Barry lied, swiping the air.

It shook its head and returned to the darkness alone.

Delivered From Darkness

Paul Rogers

It came from the darkness,
Did you hear it too?
I'm not really sure
What'll we do?

You must have heard it
As clear as day?
Am I losing my mind,
no matter what you say?

It's frightening, I'm scared,
My throat's full of lumps.
I look at my legs and arms
Covered in goosebumps.

Trembling, it's about to happen
Would it begin with a blast?
I know one thing for sure,
It's all coming way too fast.

It came from the darkness,
Like the glint from a scythe.
The scariest thing of all
The start of new life!

ARTIST

TIANA ROGERS

It Came From The Darkness

Tony Newton

It came from the darkness. It brought with it terror within its eyes. The beast was faceless, all black, only glowing red eyes. When the beast looks at you, that's when you are marked for death. Some call it the grim reaper, the dark one, Janardan, the angel of death. I have seen him before in my nightmares, forever haunting my dreams since I was a child. I always knew he was coming for me, but I never knew when death would strike. Will my soul live on forever or will he carry it straight to hell?

Eat, Martha

Matthew V. Brockmeyer

It came from the darkness of the deep forest. A fawn. A tiny baby deer, fur still dotted with white. God had sent it to us, Martha. Trembling with hunger I pounced upon it, plunging my blade into its neck. A miracle. I drank the blood and cut out its liver, devouring it raw and steaming. I've saved you some flesh, Martha, good back strap. Yes, a deer. Eat, Martha, before you die of starvation. No, I told you, I haven't seen the children, not since I saw them playing in the darkness of the deep forest. Now eat, Martha.

It Came From The Darkness

Gemma Paul

It came from the darkness
As these things often do,
It comes for your carcass,
There is nowhere to run to.

You rarely see them coming,
Not to start with anyway,
But you may hear the humming,
As you walk through the archway.

They'll always wear a mask,
Like Jason, Michael or that Texas man.
But one should never ask
Is this the bogeyman?

No matter where you run,
No matter where you hide,
You'll always be his number one,
His dream homicide.

Only the scream queen can survive,
Neve, Heather or Jamie-Lee,
So one must always strive
To be the queen bee.

ARTIST

GEMMA PAUL

Its Breath On My Sister

Mark Anthony Smith

It came from the darkness and never went back. I could not unsee it now. It creeps, on knees and gnarled palms, close to the floor. From around the bed my sister died in, I hear its nails drag against the carpet pile. She must have heard it too before the strange fit when her heart gave up. Her pupils pulled to the back of her head. I'll never forget her beneath that sickly frame – almost luminescent in the shadows. The taut skin on bones conflict with its keen eyes. Its quiet stealth makes senses prick. We'll never dream again.

Its Mind is Rage

Nick Stead

It came from the darkness, with its wings of night and horns of damnation. Bestial features snarl with hatred, and those eyes…They burn with malevolence, a window to the most twisted of souls. For its heart is evil and its mind is rage.

Crimson beads drip from clawed hands wet with blood. I can only stare at her in shock, lying broken and mutilated at my feet – its latest victim.

My head raises to meet its gaze. The red glow fades, and it retreats whence it came, my reflection human once more.

It came from the darkness. My darkness.

Let There Be Light

Laurence Saunders

It came from the darkness.
In the beginning.
'*Let there be light.*'
A garden. A tree and an apple.
Cast out in the desert.
A flood.
Lost boys and girls wander.
Trumpets sound and walls come tumbling.
A star. A celebration.
Crowds gather to listen.
Tables turned over.
A hill made of skulls.
Nails tearing flesh.
Trees are screaming.
A crown of thorns.
A cloth soaked in vinegar.
'*Why hast thou forsaken me?*'
Blood and water run apart.
A stone rolled away, the cave lies empty.
A grave robbed of life.
It came from the darkness.
'*Let there be light.*'

Michael

Matthew Cash

It came from the darkness, uncontrollable desire, one moment watching Mother washing apples for bobbing, the next walking up the stairs with his mask on and something in his hand, down the hallway to his sister's room. His own startled cry was drowned out by his sister's as he burst in on her, semi-nude and angry at her little brother's intrusion. They shared the same horror as the large knife came into view and began to stab, cut and thrust. With every slash another piece of his six-year-old mind gave into the darkness which finally began to blossom.

ARTIST

DAVID PAUL HARRIS

The Runner

David Owain Hughes

It came from the darkness and gave chase along the woodland path. Timothy Button, knowing he'd disturbed *that* spot, looked over his shoulder and saw it lumbering towards him out of the misty morning; its leafy arm was outstretched, its twig fingers reaching.

"Take up an activity?" the doctor suggested. "Exercise your demons; go back to where it began!"

The woods, he thought. *Being touching... The man and his purple root.*

Timothy couldn't face away. "Fuck off!" he said, tripping and sprawling along the floor. Before he could get back up, the demon grabbed him, dragging him into the woods.

It Came from the Darkness

A Tale of Lovecraftian and Cosmic Horror

Huw Lloyd

"It came from the darkness," those very words spoken to him nearly forty years ago. Now, as the constellations aligned above him, he held the answers to the darkest arcane questions. His dry mouth began to utter the ancient Kadathian tongue, and he began to carve. At first the pain was unbearable, the cold sting of steel against his skin. However, the power of those ancient words took hold and as his flesh fell away, he became one with the darkness, one with the cosmos.

Shriekers

Gareth Clegg

It came from the darkness, and millions fell in the carnage, flesh ripped away, leaving bloody mannequins to stumble off shrieking.

We called them Shriekers, constantly screaming as they fell upon their victims. The indiscriminate attacks ignored colour, gender and religion. They cared only about revealing the same glistening red meat within us all.

They weren't violent, infecting others with a bloody touch. The infected ripped their own faces away in shrieking madness, then sought to pass on their gift.

Two years later, we discovered the secret Zero-G lab in orbit, and its illegal bioresearch.

We'd brought this on ourselves.

Lonely Man

L.A. Lopes

It came from the darkness,
Most lonely things do.
Sensed your soft sorrow,
Your loneliness too.

It slipped between the sheets
And that space in your mind,
Projected your fears,
Created a bind.

An arm held your head,
The other your chest.
It begged for your life
As you gasped for your breath.

It then ripped at your skin,
through the blood, through the bone.
Plucked a light out,
with a smile and a moan.

It whispered,
"Finally I won't be so alone".
Then the Lonely Man, wistfully,
went off with your soul.

ARTIST

DIANE DASILVA &

LARRYSA LUPU-CHAPLIN

Demons

Tony Newton

It came from the darkness
The red reaper
The night sleeper
The creeper
The old one
The Devil's son
Lucifer rising

The soul destroyer
The cursed one
Who walks behind you
For the rest of your days
The vampire
The bat
The dormouse
The rat
The shape shifter
Who always has you in his sight
The reflection in the mirror
The fright
The last thing you see at night

The devil
The witch
The scratch you can't itch
The Monster
The beast
Your flesh it will feast
The weak are its prey
Nothing can keep the demons at bay.

That's my...

Philip Rogers & Jack Conway

It came from the darkness: a shadow of a man, half-dressed and wrapped in tattoos which covered scars both outside and in. The stench of booze clouded him like a mist, but he lacked the confidence it normally brought. He approached slowly, a quivering mass of skin and bones, desperate for a connection, longing to make amends. But his clumsy words held no power—did little to return her to me. And as he tripped over one useless word after another, my stomach churned and my fists tightened, and the voice inside my head screamed out, you're next!

Behind the Mask

Anna Laban

It came from the darkness,
Somewhere deep inside.
Where it has festered for years,
Now has nowhere to hide.
No one else could see it,
No one else knew.
Blackness invading the soul,
Hiding all that was true.
A little latent secret,
Just for one,
Waiting silently,
Like a loaded gun.
Loneliness wrapped around,
Like a bow on a gift.
Suffocating and overpowering,
The darkness wouldn't lift.
Everything within,
Being twisted inside out.
No escape from this monster,
No point trying to shout.
Drip, drip, drip,
The redness hit the floor.
Still invisible to others,
The darkness was no more.

ARTIST

ANNA LABAN

Poppy Dog

Lee Franklin

It came from the darkness and tore at my heart with worry. Poppy's desperate barks fading into a mewling whine. The crunching gold leaves fracture and disintegrate into squelching mud as I find her flailing, exhausted in the bog.

Reaching for her collar, a gnarled and rotting hand erupts from the sludge, grabbing my wrist like a vice. I slip and slide in the muck as it pulls me in. More hands claw out of the mire, tearing at my body as they drag me deep into the suffocating earth. The bog's crushing embrace strangles my unheard screams into silence.

Mr President

P.J. Blakey-Novis

It came from the darkness of worlds beyond ours, that lone craft of obsidian black and its sole inhabitant. But one invader was all it would take. Taking on a human guise, the creature came to rule, by deception and division, unable to hide his black soul as he took his place in a house of white. The dark one quickly took control of the Earth, destroying any who stood against him, using black magic to gain a loyal following. Worshipped as a god by the foolish, the world stood by helplessly as the final bombs began to fall.

Mother. R.I.P.

Martin W. Payne

It came from the darkness. I felt it creeping up from the corner of the room.

My mother's living room - now only occupied by myself after the extended family and friends had departed. My mother would have loved to be present at her wake, but maybe, in a way, she was.

It felt like she was still there. I felt the weight of years on me, my memory of her still lurking around me, in the shadows, behind my chair. I shivered, suddenly feeling cold, daring to turn, to look behind and see... nothing. Hearing her say *goodnight*.

Light

J.C. Michael

It came from the darkness. A pinprick of flickering light approaching at a barely perceptible speed. It was impossible to gauge the passage of time in the smothering black, but hours must've passed as the light gradually drew near. Identifiable now as a flame, dancing in a breeze I could not feel, I was certain it was a candle. It inched toward me, proving my suspicion correct, allowing me to see the outline of the hand which held it, but nothing more. An eternity passed, the flame reaching my face, only to be extinguished by a whisper... "Even angels die sometimes".

It Came From The Darkness

Pablo Raybould (Shooting Lodge Productions)

It came from the darkness of its mother's womb. A jagged, mutated form with broken bones that tore as it was pulled into the light. This vile, hate-filled adult-formed baby scowled as it surveyed the maternity unit while mother bled out. Silence. The pain it screamed with was nothing to what it would serve before it could be terminated. A nurse reluctantly... cautiously, took the 'thing' to swaddle. How it took the scalpel into its deformed fingers no-one recalls. Its first grin was when it plunged the blade, bursting her eye and through to the soft frontal lobe.

Reader, Alone

Laurence Saunders

It came from the darkness…

At first you didn't notice. You were too busy reading.

The air feels close, like a thunderstorm waiting to break. A sour taste, like glass, rests on the back of your tongue. Your eyes skim the words on the page, trying to make sense of them. You feel the weight of the story in your hands. There's a smell of metal, like old pennies.

Hot breath on the back of your neck. Something else is there with you. You turn your head.

Blood spatters onto the page, scattering the words like spiders. The final punctuation.

Melancholy

David Green

It came from the darkness and found a home in my brain.

My creeping despair nourished it, and it grew fat. It dug its claws in my grey matter and refused to let go. When I open my mouth, it uses my voice. As I dream it reveals its deepest desires.

I drift through existence. A shadow on my soul twists and writhes. I think of myself and imagine black ichor flowing through my veins.

I look at you, but I don't see. It looks through them as it eats my insides. Day by day I'm less, and it grows.

Dredge

Reece Connolly

It came from the darkness. From the black sucking mud of the old riverbed. Now - with the heavy rain, the flooding - encouraged upwards. A dog-walker spotted it; something unusual in the rushing waters. They called the police: 'It's something big. Metal-looking. Some sort of box...?' A digger came. They shone floodlights, set to work. Moving the dirt, the jagged rocks. People gathered, despite the storm. Watching the long box being heaved onto the bank. Inside the iron coffin, sealed with silver, the witch stirred - pale eyes flickered, screwed-up heart flushing with blood, teeth chattering, ready to feast.

Siren Song

Cortney Palm

It came from the darkness
Such a haunting sound
Uttered from the melancholic lips
Of the lost yet never found
– a manifestation of –
of what, exactly?

No mortal words seem
Fit enough to describe
The otherworldly theme
Of this eerie lullaby
- a maleficence -
Pleasure or pain?

A mistaken "I am" identity
Breathed by a false prophet
Is there a point to reality?
Just stop it!
- existential -
Is there a point?!

O' curse the cacophony of sound
The she of all the sheep
That draws me down, down, down
To the depths where
Caught souls
Dance fettered
And thus
Forever weep

Sweet Dream

Tony Sands

It came from the darkness, a clickety-clack that startled Cassie from her snooze.

"Hello?" She brushed chills from her arms and stood up, blearily peering into the shadows. Nothing.

"Very funny, you got me," she muttered, lacking conviction. A minute passed, two, but only silence replied.

You were dreaming, she told herself, though she had a knot of dread in her stomach. Cursing her fears, she checked on the baby who was sleeping quietly in his cot. She smiled as his little lips parted. Clickety-clack came the sound and a dark, spindly leg pushed out of his mouth. Cassie screamed.

Tavern Whispers

Mark Cassell

It came from the darkness reeking of seaweed and rotted meat.

Edmund stumbled from the cave mouth, tripped and sprawled across pebbles. His forehead cracked against rock. The rush of water and pounding footfalls urged him to scramble up. He blindly grasped at slick limestone. Blinking sticky blood, he turned.

And squinted into the glistening hulk of the very creature he was there to debunk.

A thing of limbs, of clacking pincers, scraping claws, and swaying pseudopods dripping smoky acid… it lunged.

His scream met its roar, its ravaging embrace.

His death became yet another whisper in the local tavern.

The Brooklyn Butcher

Monster Smith

It came from the darkness...slashing at my blouse under the grimacing glow of the moon. His blade struck bone, filleting my breast like a seasoned veteran. Pain coursed through my entire body and I hit the pavement, swallowing teeth as I gasped for air. *Momma always said there'd be days like these,* I thought, gurgling blood.

"Sorry to interrupt, folks," blurted the anchorman. "But I'm told that Chief Lotus has just called a press conference concerning the deranged policeman - which we will bring to you next, live from the steps of City Hall, when we return after these messages."

The Gestation Of Hate

Mark Steensland

It came from the darkness
Between the cypress trees
The thing with red eyes
And lips of rotting leaves
With swamp water dripping
From its moss-covered hide
Step by dragging step
Growing closer like the tide
This shadow-born beast
Lives beyond time and space
Forever fighting the light
In search of a dark place
The mind of a killer serves well
The heart of a bigot, too
Like sun to the sunflower
Any black moon will do
Once settled, it breeds
An unholy mother
Giving birth to more
Sisters and brothers
That come from the dark
To make yet another.

ARTIST

ART AUTOPSY

Soul Eater

J. A. Sullivan

It came from the darkness,
Beneath bridge moonshadow
Onyx eyes in rotting flesh, bone splinter crown
Wading through frigid river rapids
Summoned forth by despair and grief
Hungering for my fractured spirit.
"Feed me your pain," the soul eater wailed.
Plank edge beneath my feet, cold steel railing in my grasp,
Anguish, torment, guilt spilled down in a torrent of screams
Devoured by the ravenous maw below.
Purged.
Tiny fingers tugged on broken heartstrings
Clumsy bunny loops and shoelace knots
Protecting my remaining shard of hope.
"Until tomorrow," the soul eater said,
Licking fangs, sloshing back from whence it came.

Schooled

Laurence Saunders

It came from the darkness. A thought, once shapeless, took form. The blue light of the computer screen caught in my glasses. Ideas seeded then flowered over early hours. Taunts in the schoolyard withered on the vine.

Blood and soil.

Here I sit, on the floor of the refectory, my boots and hands sticky. My ears ring - eeeeeeeeeeeee - deafened by the gunshots, a bell that will never stop tolling. My classmates' broken bodies, shattered skulls, surround me. My shoulder is bruised from the recoil of the gun. Someone is sobbing. What have I done?

I am the darkness.

The Chudail (Witch)

Maya & Singh Lall

It came from the darkness. That is the only explanation I have.

Who watches a videotape without a label? Only one thing appeared on that grainy VHS. In Pakistan they call it a Bakhtuk, here in India the woman with feet facing backwards is a chudail. Her white eyes and black hair appear pure but hold a power darker than you could comprehend.

He pressed play and she appeared, causing his hair to turn white and sending his mind into the abyss.

Lurking in the darkest corner of Hell lies the Bollywood VHS. An obsolete monstrosity awaiting its next victim.

The Creature

Lou Yardley

It came from the darkness, but I didn't see it at first. I just heard scratching. It watched me night after night, learning my habits.

Then it appeared with its six rows of teeth and a dozen legs. The creature blinked at me with its one red eye. It was the size of my hand, but I knew it was dangerous. Scuttling at speed, it climbed up my body, forcing its way into my mouth.

It controls me now. When I resist, its six rows of teeth tear into me. So I do what it wants.

We've killed so many.

Traffic Incident

Dale Parnell

"It came from the darkness, what do you think that means?"

"I don't know, Philips, people say odd things after car accidents."

The ambulance pulled away, siren screaming, leaving PCs Stone and Philips on the scene, waiting for the recovery lorry. Philips was about to speak when the car battery suddenly died, killing the blue flashing lights and plunging them into darkness.

"Stone?"

A gagged scream, then hot, rancid breath hit the back of his neck, followed by the wet crunch of breaking bones.

"From the darkness," Philips whispered, as a leathery, clawed hand closed around his face and squeezed.

This Is Your Punishment

Tori Romero

It came from the darkness and trapped her forever. While packing her late great aunt's belongings, Samantha stumbled upon a creepy porcelain doll that resembled her perfectly. Out of curiosity, she brought it home. She could feel its eyes following her every move and threw it in the closet.

In the middle of the night, a ghostly figure whispered into her ear, "This is your punishment for never visiting me."

Samantha screamed but it was too late. When her mom opened the door, Samantha was no longer there. In her place was the doll, with a note that read *HELP*.

Who's There?

Arthur M Harper

It came from the darkness, a guttural, rasping groan.

I freeze. My foot hovers, mid-step. My breath catches.

I hear the groan again. A curtain flutters, the window shattered from outside.

Claws seize my ankle. I recoil, gasping in horror. It crawls on its chest, fleshy ribbons trailing from the gaping hole where the legs should be. The stench of raw meat is overpowering.

"Help...meeee."

It's yanked backwards into the darkness. A crunch silences the groan.

I flip the light switch. The beast grins, chops dripping with the burglar's blood. It gratefully accepts a scratch behind the ear.

"Good lad."

The Truth

Debbie Rochon

It came from the darkness. I held my flashlight steady. The movement of the decomposing glob crackled the brittle fall leaves in its path. I had buried it with such force. It rotted for thirty years. The very existence of it caused me sickness that I treated with endless futile remedies. It was now in the road in front of me. I knew it would come for me. No negotiating. No running. No avoidance. No second burial. I was now face to face with the creature of my making and it was going to kill me. It was The Truth.

Your Blood, My Love

Jason McFiggins

It came from the darkness,
my life.
Bursts, spatter,
this once red ocean emptied.
Cold
moans and cries throughout me,
ghosts trapped until dried out.

I hunt darkness, looking
for you,
the rush of the red glide inside.
Still, the darkness
stays beneath the skin,
spreading from
the empty fountain in my chest,
thump
thump
thump, from memory.

It came from the darkness,
my life.
You drown me by
the minute, when I bite.
I carry you under my skin, so I may live
while you die, becoming
like me.
Our lives remain
a memory. Our death
will last
forever.

Donor

David Owain Hughes

It came from the darkness of the corridor and eased the door open. Terry, bent over the provided skin mag, wanking, looked up at the stockinged legs before him and smiled.

Finally! he thought. *With all the times I've been coming here to donate my love-muck, leaving the door unlatched, a nurse walks in and makes my day!* Pre-come dribbled out of his dick, his eyes climbing the slender, uniform-wrapped body.

Terry's cock shrivelled, his eyes latching onto a gaping mouth filled with razors. "Blood giver too!" it screeched, ripping his prick off and placing a beaker to the fountain.

The Littlest Creature

Tony Mardon

It came from the darkness
Because it thought it should,
Had stayed too long behind the light
But got close as it could…

Now,
this little creature
Didn't really feature as he dwelt
upon the wrong side of the tree.
Until the day he leered at a door
that had appeared and in the lock he
turned the rusty key.

How proudly did he stand having
entered our own land,
No longer in the dark but
In the light.
He asked me for your name,
so I gave it, all the same.

He said he's going to visit you tonight.

ARTIST

TONY MARDON

Never Ever

Seán Breathnach

It came from the darkness - a pitch dark corner in my room. I don't recall it being there before. I've always slept with a light on. Just one light back then. I thought one was enough.

Why was that corner so completely dark? I got out of bed and walked over to it. My shadow touched the darkness and IT moved - from the darkness into my own shadow. Now it's with me all the time, living in my shadow.

That's why I sleep with so many lights on every night. There can never be a shadow here. Never ever.

Death in Paradise

David Owain Hughes

It came from the darkness and swallowed him forever. His laughter was profound, his mind a melting pot of guilt and unravelling thoughts of the life, wife and children that he'd left behind; suicide beckoned from the fringes of reality in this lonely, lovely sanctuary.

"Run, but no hide," he jabbered, rocking on his heels. "Your problems are your luggage."

The sun outside his veranda window winked off the razor he held. Timothy gargled his prayers, his blood spraying, as he tried to flee to another land of hope and peace.

This time, he thought, *the pain will go away...*

They're Still Out Here

Matt Doyle

It came from the darkness. And we knew, even then, that something was wrong. The war that sent us fleeing into the oceans is a distant memory for the youngsters, but people like us still remember. When we close our eyes at night, we can still hear the sounds those *things* made when they came down from the sky.

This is like that. But something about it draws us. Even seeing the huge, shrieking serpent waiting for us, we can't stop heading towards it.

Oh, God.

Tell our families we love them. And tell everyone else... they're still out here.

Bad Idea

Dave Jeffery

It came from the darkness of his mind, not as a fleeting thought but something that had matured over time; a concept so terrible, he'd buried it. But rather than remain entombed, the idea grew into a restless spirit.

What lived in his mind is a concept, a word, an act; caged for now, but the lock is loose, the notion nudging at the door, testing resistance.

On the morning the thought escaped and became the act, he said it over and over, louder and louder, so that it could be heard above his wife's desperate, hideous screams.

"Murder! Murder!"

Pure Evil

David Gaskin

It came from the darkness. The formless flowing, the putrescent smell, the sharpened teeth and narrowed eyes.

It had entered from the air ducts, relentlessly moving to its goal, slithering and continuing with its barely perceptible mewling and screeching.

It carried on, despite the shouts and cries, travelling to complete its one aim - obsessive in its mission.

The final moments brought the greatest horrors. The creature entering the room and becoming aware of us.

The blood, the screams and the final pleasure. Its death was beautiful and I smiled to myself. It came from the darkness. Evil brought us forth.

Creature of the Night

Alexander Churchyard

It came from the darkness, that foul, loathsome creature of the night. It leaves death in its wake, the viscera of its prey a grotesque reminder of its presence. This most unholy creature lies dormant during daylight. At night I am woken to the sounds of its foul cries. My land is befouled, I am unable to cross my threshold without being stained by its mark. To invite it into my home would be to place myself under its influence, for they are insidious and able to make man do their bidding.

Name thyself demon!

Its amulet reads…Mittens.

Hexed Man's Lament

Clifford Beal

It came from the darkness.
It came for my soul.
It came unbidden, unwanted, unchecked.
It came from a place: my corrupted heart's hole.

From the well of my being, poison rose up,
A foreign invader, stealing my sleep.
An insult, once I uttered, too late to withdraw,
Now, at last, I see the revenge she will reap.

My fingers are growing;
I feel my bones crack.
A monster within me arises,
My huge eyes pierce the black.

It came from the darkness;
That much may be true.
But now, my dear friend,
It is coming for you.

It Came From The Darkness

C.M. Angus

It came to dream of those fool enough to meddle with Old Magick.

It watched Sophie for years — watched and slumbered. But since her attunement, everything had changed — *now it could taste her.*

Ever since then, she had locked the door and turned the world away — *Why tolerate the banal when there was power like this?*

Mouthing the words, Sophie clumsily drew its name symbol.

Foolish girl...

Feeling heat and resistance between her palms, Sophie poured all of her intention into what progressively became a glowing ball of energy.

It was then that it awoke...

Till Death Do Us Part

Dale Parnell

It came from the darkness, your voice a dry, coarse whisper.

"Sasha?"

I tried so many times to tell you it was over, but you wouldn't listen. And now you've dragged your corpse out of the mud, as if that proves something.

Till death do us part, that's the deal. Well, you're dead honey, and I'll make damn sure that you stay that way.

They start building the new housing estate soon, plenty of foundations to choose from. If two feet of dirt couldn't keep you down, let's see what you make of two-hundred tons of concrete, bricks and mortar.

ARTIST
CONG NGUYEN

Split

P.J. Blakey-Novis

It came from the darkness, the pit of my mind. That section filled with all the trauma and pain. *It* had a voice, unlike my own, but clear and commanding. My therapist would have said the trauma of my past had 'escaped' from the metaphorical box we'd worked so hard to trap it in, that it had fractured my essence and split my personality. But, being stuck in the same head as *It*, I had no way of knowing if this was true. I just had to accept it, like an unwanted roommate. Even when it told me to kill.

It Came From The Darkness

Charlie Steeds

It came from the darkness of the infinite ocean floor. Henry's safety line. Snapped. Floating limp, like a headless serpent. That'd alerted us to danger below.

Why me!? For this doomed rescue mission... Soon came the red fish, swimming in groups. Wait... not fish! Chunks... Of torn, gnawed flesh!

Henry. My insides twisted! What'd Henry found!?!

Then, air bubbles, alerting me to life... swimming up from the blackness!

I glimpsed, for a second...WHY!? Spider-crabs? Couldn't be... One thousand twisting legs on each side...claws...those luminous suckers!!

I gasped my last breath as they reached me, and in an instant... Red fish.

The Skull of Wrath

V.Castro

It came from the darkness of the empty eye socket where the eels gather to nest. Their sharp teeth had long cleaned the skull from all remaining flesh. The Skull of Wrath fell into the water during the last witch hunt. Silent and cold but not lonely, for the eels created new life in the empty and cosy space.

Graciela fished with her father for years. She worried about his declining health and his constant concern for their well-being. As she held a strange, algae covered skull in her hands, she had the premonition their luck was about to change.

Not Unpunished

Tracy Allen

It came from the darkness,
The smell of meat, red and raw
Peeled from long, white bones
And crammed past splintered teeth
Into a masticating maw.

We raise our weapon,
One of earthbound wood and ore,
Quicksilver fast,
A clean cut aside,
Teeth-torn flesh and jaw.

This is not the end, instead
Conformed to extraordinary law,
A visit from the spirit
Who became the monster,
A demanding, omnipotent caw.

Pleading for release
Into our private, mindful yaw,
Omniscient, omnipresent,
Needling, pleading,
No escape from its incessant draw.

Serial Killer Soliloquy

Danni Winn

It came from the darkness... thoughts, compulsions that have continued to consume and dictate my life. They ignite an uncommon departure from empathy and thoroughly shred any ties to what can label me as actually human. I have watched you for weeks and noted your movements. You don't know it yet, but you will be mine. I will play in your blood and revel in your "mysterious disappearance" broadcast on the news as my crooked smile and cold gaze center on the ring I will sever from your delicate finger. You don't know it yet, but you are now mine.

Beguiled

Craig Fisher

It came from the darkness, deep within the forest. The woods themselves were black and dense, yet emanated the hollowness of a cavernous void. But those eyes, dear God, those piercing eyes. Radiating such malice, reverberating with an inhumane history of horrors. I try to look away, run, fly. But feel trapped, held down on the spot, incomprehensibly beguiled.

Like fragments of a broken mirror, when pieced back together I begin to understand the truth... I am shocked and appalled to realise I am looking at my own reflection. How callous of the beast to force me to acknowledge this.

It Came From The Darkness

Helen Laban

It came from the darkness, a deep sense of fear.
I could feel it upon me, as shadows grew near.

Dark and alone, cold surrounds me.
I try to hide, but fear overwhelms me.

Demons, goblins, ghouls of the night.
They're coming to get me, I quiver with fright.

My heart is pounding, I shudder in fear.
Menacing cackles are all I hear.

As monsters surround me, there's nowhere to go.
I trip and I stumble, falling down low.

As they move in closer, they grab and they pull me.
They drag me along, and slowly consume me.

ARTIST

NATASHA NEALE

Black Eyed Child

Tom Lee Rutter

It came from the darkness and knocked on the front door. I remember the knock was firm but spaced apart – like it moved in an ethereal time of its own. It was late and I was startled awake. Frightened, but in a hypnotic state atwix the waking life and another – I unlocked and opened the door. The child stared back at me with its black vacuous eyes and reached out its arms. I never saw the growing face of what was lost to me, but I knew, I just knew, that his would have been mine.

Under the Cabinet

Debra Lamb

It came from the darkness, a scrawny hand shakily reaches out from under the kitchen cabinet to snatch up a small apple that had fallen off the table. The movement catches the attention of a small child, who crawls closer to the cabinet, placing a piece of his biscuit next to it. The child giggles with delight as the creature reaches out from under the cabinet to take the biscuit. The child lays its head on the wooden floor, locking eyes with the creature, coaxing him to come out. The two sit in the kitchen eating apples and biscuits, laughing.

Chaos

Danni Winn

It came from the darkness. From the night sky that bore no stars or moon. On a cool, fall evening something came crashing into our orbit. Igniting the dense sky with a whirlwind of mystery; emitting sparks of magenta and a motion that shook not only my soul, but the very foundation on which I stood - I helplessly watched as something greater than ourselves simultaneously illuminated our earth while casting it in a shadow. Chaos and colors surrounded us all, with many succumbing to complete madness after learning of and accepting our insignificance in the universe. It was fate.

Contributor Bios

P.J. Blakey-Novis is the author of several collections of short horror stories and co-founder of Red Cape Publishing.

Matt Doyle - Award-winning hybrid genre author, pop culture blogger and indie game developer.

Martin W. Payne: Accountant, Freemason, Actor, Producer, Director, Writer.

Mark Anthony Smith was born in Hull, East Yorkshire. You can find out more at www.markanthonysmith.com

Alexander Churchyard, filmmaker from Southend-on-Sea. Co-Director of I Scream on the Beach!

Gareth Clegg lives in make-believe worlds somewhere in the dark spaces between science fiction, horror and fantasy - author. to/garethclegg

Jamie Evans is a writer and filmmaker in Essex with stories published in various collections; "The Librarian", "Shell-Shocked" and "Aftermath"

John Ryan Howard is an Irish film & television actor who has starred in two horror feature films - 'Beyond The Woods' & 'Gate Way.'

David Paul Harris is the publisher of Mandatory Midnight, an eMagazine dedicated to discovering new and upcoming authors of horror and experimental fiction. He provides authors with a platform from which to gain a following and illustrations for each story published. Visit Mandatory Midnight at https://www. davidpaulharris.com/

Matthew Cash is head witch doctor at Burdizzo Books and has loads of stuff available on Amazon & Audible.

Eric LaRocca's horror fiction has been published in various literary journals and anthologies in the U.S. and abroad.

Maya Lall is a 15-year-old horror fan like her father ***Singh Lall*** who is a supporter of independent horror and they have combined to write a tale based on Indian folklore.

Huw Lloyd is a writer, director and host of the Undead Wookie Podcast.

Peter Germany is a Word Wrangler from the United Kingdom, you can find out more at petergermany.com

Violet Castro is a Mexican American writer originally from Texas now residing in the UK. www.vvcastro.com

Charlie Steeds is a Writer/Director of horror movies (An English Haunting, A Werewolf in England, and many more) made through his independent production company Dark Temple Motion Pictures.

Chris Lloyd - I write short stories, monologues and plays plus Stand Up poetry i.e. I stand up and shout a lot!

Lou Yardley is an indie author and gorehound from the UK. She likes monsters, blood, and guts… but mostly she just loves a good story.

Tracy Allen is the co-owner of horror review site PopHorror.com along with ***Tori Danielle Romero***.

Clifford Beal has published several fantasy novels for Solaris Books as well as short fiction horror in Weirdbook quarterly.

Cong Nguyen is a freelance storyboard artist and illustrator, working mainly in film and commercial, and sometimes children book illustration.

Tony Sands is a father, a writer, a wearer of hats.

Jason McFiggins has done social media for Death House and Camp Dread, and has been writing about horror for MorbidlyBeautiful. com since 2016, including a monthly column called Video Rewind.

Anna Laban, artist, owner of Designs at Heart and teacher.

Alain Elliott is a writer, blogger and lifelong horror fanatic.

Nick Stead spends his days prowling the darker side of fiction, and is best known for his Hybrid series (werewolf horror) - http://author.to/nickstead

Bill 'Bloody Bill' Pon is a filmmaker, hauntrepreneur and Guitar Slayer from Wild West Texas.

Owen Townend is a writer of speculative short fiction, hailing from Huddersfield.

Tom Lee Rutter is a filmmaker based in Worcs, UK. His films include Bella In The Wych Elm and the upcoming The Pocket Film Of Superstitions.

Craig Fisher is a filmmaker from Wales, UK, specialising in the LGBTQ+ and Horror Genres.

L.A. Lopes is an anxiety ridden, film obsessed creative, who spends an obscene amount of time in dark rooms writing about the adventures of the fictional people that live in her head.

Diane DaSilva is a tornado-chasing, ghost-hunting, truth-seeking adventurer and animal activist.

Larrysa Lupu-Chaplin is a colourful seeker of truth and knowledge, who braves through the veils of illusion with a passion for true liberation of people and animals.

Roma Gray writes what she refers to as "Trick-or-Treat Thrillers", stories with a spooky, creepy, Halloween feel to them.

Mike T. Lyddon is an award-winning writer, producer, director and special makeup effects artist whose latest film WITCH TALES is currently in distribution and can be found on horroranthologymovies.com.

Danni Winn is a lifelong genre fan turned passionate horror journalist and writer.

Peter Hearn directed horror feature 'Scrawl' starring Daisy Ridley & wrote Punks v Gremlins proof of concept 'Dead Air'.

Debra Lamb is an award-winning actor and published author, whose work, both on the screen and on the page, has been chilling audiences for over 30 years!

Chisto Healy has been writing since childhood, but he only started following his dreams and writing full time in 2020. On top of the award nominated self-published novels from his earlier days, he now has over one hundred published stories.

Monster Smith is an author, writer, film producer, podcast host, cryptozoologist, and mixed martial artist from Chandler, Arizona.

Also from Red Cape Publishing

Anthologies:

Elements of Horror Book One: Earth
Elements of Horror Book Two: Air
Elements of Horror Book Three: Fire
Elements of Horror Book Four: Water
A is for Aliens: A to Z of Horror Book One
B is for Beasts: A to Z of Horror Book Two
C is for Cannibals: A to Z of Horror Book Three
D is for Demons: A to Z of Horror Book Four
E is for Exorcism: A to Z of Horror Book Five
F is for Fear: A to Z of Horror Book Six

Short Story Collections:

Embrace the Darkness by P.J. Blakey-Novis
Tunnels by P.J. Blakey-Novis
The Artist by P.J. Blakey-Novis
Karma by P.J. Blakey-Novis
The Place Between Worlds by P.J. Blakey-Novis
Short Horror Stories by P.J. Blakey-Novis
Keep It Inside & Other Weird Tales by Mark Anthony Smith

Novelettes:

The Ivory Tower by Antoinette Corvo

Novellas:

Four by P.J. Blakey-Novis
Three by P.J. Blakey-Novis
Dirges in the Dark by Antoinette Corvo

Novels:

Madman Across the Water by Caroline Angel
The Curse Awakens by Caroline Angel
The Vegas Rift by David F. Gray
The Broken Doll by P.J. Blakey-Novis
Shattered Pieces by P.J. Blakey-Novis

Children's Books:

The Little Bat That Could by Gemma Paul
The Mummy Walks at Midnight by Gemma Paul
Grace & Bobo: The Trip to the Future by Peter Blakey-Novis

Follow Red Cape Publishing

www.redcapepublishing.com
www.facebook.com/redcapepublishing
www.twitter.com/redcapepublish
www.instagram.com/redcapepublishing
www.pinterest.co.uk/redcapepublishing
www.patreon.com/redcapepublishing

Printed in Great Britain
by Amazon

49061128R00077